The Pumpkin Project

The Pumpkin Project

KATIE SMITH

Illustrated by Sarah Jennings

Hodder
Children's
Books

HODDER CHILDREN'S BOOKS

First published in Great Britain in 2000 by Hodder and Stoughton Ltd
This edition published in 2016 by Hodder and Stoughton Ltd

1 3 5 7 9 10 8 6 4 2

Text copyright ©Katie Smith 2016
Illustrations copyright ©Sarah Jennings 2016
Inner cover photo by Luke Smith

A CIP catalogue record for this book is available from the British Library.

ISBN 9781 444 93691 9

Printed and bound in Great Britain by Clays Ltd, St Ives plc

The paper and board used in this book are made from wood from responsible
sources

Hodder Children's Books
An imprint of Hachette Children's Group
Part of Hodder and Stoughton
Carmelite House, 50 Victoria Embankment, London, EC4Y 0DZ

An Hachette UK Company
www.hachette.co.uk

To my finches.
Here's one to tick off the list.

ONE

Did you know that the largest pumpkin
ever to exist in Great Britain was grown
by twins Ian and Stuart Paton in a town
called Pennington? It took over six months
to grow and measured well over a metre
tall!

You can probably look up this fact on the Internet or in one of the books in your school library. You'll undoubtedly be able to find a picture of the twins standing by the humungous orange beast and smiling proudly at their giant vegetable creation.

But what you won't know is that this interesting fact is, in fact, not a fact at all.

The largest pumpkin ever to exist in Great Britain was actually grown by an eight-year-old girl called Lottie Parsons. It measured over two metres tall (about the size of two baby elephants standing on top of one another!) and took exactly twenty-seven days to grow.

There are no photographs of this giant creation. There is no evidence to say it ever existed at all. In fact, there are only three people who have even seen this extraordinarily enormous vegetable.

I expect you would like to know why

an eight-year-old girl would even want to grow a supersized pumpkin in the first place. Well, it's a long story, but it starts with Lottie in her least favourite place.

School.

4

'Only fifteen minutes late this morning,
Lottie! What an achievement!' called Mrs
Murray across the classroom, as Lottie
hung up her coat and bag and stumbled
towards her seat with her pencil case.

Lottie heard a snigger from across the

classroom and checked to see whether she'd tucked her skirt into her knickers again like yesterday.

Like most eight-year-olds, Lottie struggled to drag herself out of bed every morning and ended up being late for school most days. She didn't mind school; in truth she loved the thrill of exploring new ideas and learning cool stuff. If her mum could ever be bothered to attend parents' evening, Lottie's teacher would be able to explain that her daughter was a bright and capable child. Nevertheless, Lottie remained unenthusiastic about school and could pinpoint the two main reasons why.

The first thing that made Maplebrook Primary so intolerable was Penelope Pembleton-Puce.

I use the word 'thing' purposely, as this is exactly the right word to describe

7

the girl in question. Penelope Pembleton-Puce had a face that reminded Lottie of one of those little wooden elves one often finds dangling from a Christmas tree. She was slightly chubby, with tiny, piercing-blue eyes; small, protruding ears; sharp, defined eyebrows; and a thin grin. Every feature of Penelope's face was abnormally small, aside from her nose, which was abnormally large and caused her to snort like a pig whenever she laughed, most of the time at Lottie. Her hair was always pulled back into a French plait which looked as neat at the end of the school day as it did at the beginning, the exact opposite of Lottie's unruly mane of thick brown curls.

Penelope had a habit of over-pronouncing the A sound, which often made her sound like she was singing in an opera rather than having a normal conversation.

For some reason, Penelope took great delight in making Lottie feel horrible. Last year, when Penelope brought in home-made biscuits for her birthday, Lottie was the only person who didn't receive one. Lottie's teacher, Mrs Murray, had tried to make her feel better by offering Lottie a Slimmer's

World chocolate-coated rice cake. While Lottie sat in the corner trying to lick the chocolate off something that tasted like cardboard, the rest of her classmates feasted on indulgent cookies.

Despite her meanness towards Lottie, Penelope was never told off by any of the staff at Maplebrook Primary. Mrs Murray was a kind teacher but, like a lot of Lottie's classmates (and all of the other teachers for that matter), she tried to stay on the good side of Penelope at all times. Mr Pembleton-Puce – Penelope's father – was well known for the special gifts that he handed out to teachers at the end of term.

Here's a little secret about teachers that you may not know. Most of them do not like children very much.

However, teachers *do* like gifts.

There is probably nothing more thrilling for a teacher than the prospect of receiving an expensive end-of-year thank-you pressie from a child in their class. It is the highlight of their year.

Mrs Murray was looking forward to receiving her iPad and spa day vouchers from the Pembleton-Puce family – so very much, in fact, that she frequently ignored Penelope's cruel treatment of others.

Penelope was the polar opposite of Lottie; where the former was rich, the latter was poor. Penelope arrived at school every day on time, looking perfect and well cared for; Lottie trudged in late, in an untidy state. Lottie was intelligent. Penelope was not.

Penelope's parents tried to make up for her lack of intelligence by throwing money at virtually everything she did at school. They encouraged their daughter to make friends by bringing in expensive gifts for them on their birthdays, and when it came to school projects, Penelope would always win the class prize because Mrs Pembleton-Puce would hire experts to create spectacular masterpieces for her end-of-term presentation.

Last term, when their topic was Fire

and Ice, Penelope danced in an iridescent
leotard around a metre-tall working
volcano that spewed out smoke and lava.

As she performed the splits, the papier mâché mountain melted away to reveal an ice sculpture of a baby polar bear. Unsurprisingly, she walked away with first prize.

The end-of-term project was the second reason Lottie hated school. The last day before the Christmas holidays, all pupils were herded into the assembly hall and made to present a project they had been working on at home. It was such an important part of the year that each child received an explanatory letter to take home to their family, along with an invitation to witness the projects at the end of the year.

Those with parents who cared about their child's reputation made some effort to help produce something that their children could be proud of.

Because her mum was unwilling to participate, last year Lottie ended up preparing something embarrassing about the Antarctic on scraps of paper that she found in the kitchen cupboard.

There was, of course, a prize for the winner of each year group, but Lottie knew she would never have a chance to win anything while up against the likes of Penelope. There was really no point in her trying, but Mrs Murray insisted over and over again, like a squawking parrot:

'At Maplebrook Primary we do not give up. Determination and imagination are the keys to success!'

Lottie would have to produce something.

The school project was being announced today.

She had five weeks.

THREE

'Big and Small!' moaned Lottie to her classmate William in the playground at lunchtime. 'Why do they always have such stupid, boring titles?'

The project had been announced earlier that morning and the playground was buzzing with conversation. As usual, Year Three had been given a title that contained opposites, to allow them to come up with more ideas. As you may have already guessed, this term's topic was Big and Small.

Lottie was right; it *was* a little boring.

'You can interpret the theme in any way you like,' Mr Dulland, the headteacher, had told the sea of eager faces. 'As long as it fits in some way, anything will be accepted.'

The class had spent the rest of the morning brainstorming different words for big and small, and researching ideas on the computer to give them inspiration. Penelope had whipped out her mobile phone almost immediately after assembly to Facetime her mother to discuss ideas. All the way through to breaktime, Penelope boasted to her classmates about what she was going to do to win. Lottie had spent most of this time thinking about what she was going to have for lunch.

'I think Big and Small is quite a good title,' said William. 'I'm going to research the world's largest and the world's smallest animals, and make a book of facts about them.'

William Winkleman, a timid little

blond boy in Lottie's year, was the only person at school she could call a friend. They had bonded last year when Lottie stuck up for William because Penelope was teasing him about being short.

William's father was a vet, with an obsession for collecting unusual animals. Last term, William confided in Lottie that his dad kept a fully grown ostrich in the garden and had recently become the proud owner of a baby porcupine.

Understandably, William was following in his father's footsteps and he was turning into an animal collector too. His seventh birthday party was held at their local zoo, where he spent most of the day trying to lure an emperor penguin into his rucksack with a digestive biscuit.

'Yes, a book about the largest and the smallest animals of the world,' he repeated through a mouth full of cheese puffs. 'My dad will probably help me to make some kind of demonstration model too.'

Some help would be nice, thought Lottie, guessing that she would get none when she handed her mum the letter that very afternoon.

She was right. Again.

'Why should I be bothered with some stupid project for school anyway?' Mrs Parsons screeched venomously. 'I don't get paid to teach you! That's what the teachers should be doing. When *I* was at school you did sums from the blackboard! When *I* was at school, *we* didn't bother with any of that project rubbish. I don't see why *you* should be able to have fun when *I* didn't.'

'Vegetables,' Grandpa grumbled from his chair.

Mrs Parsons whipped her head towards her father-in-law. 'Oh, be quiet, you stupid old fool,' she bellowed. 'You haven't got vegetables for tea. You've got liver and onion stew.'

Another low grumble came from Grandpa. If you've ever tasted liver and onion stew, you'd know why Grandpa was grumbling.

'I know, Gramps,' said Lottie with a sigh.

'Pah! Big and Small. Stupid title. What rubbish will they come up with next!' Lottie's mum ranted to herself, screwed up the letter and threw it into the dustbin. 'It's just another excuse for those lazy teachers to sit on their big fat bums and drink coffee all day!'

Lottie couldn't help but stare at her own mother's rather large bottom and think about the phrase involving a pot and kettle that she had learned at school recently.

'Anyway, I haven't got time to talk about a silly little project with you. I've got to finish this zone on Liquorice Legend. I've been stuck on Level 261 for five days and Sylvia next door has overtaken me!'

Mrs Parsons slumped in the chair next to the television with her eyes glued to her mobile phone.

She stuffed a chocolate bar into her mouth with one hand and moved the thumb of her other hand across the screen of the device, which kept making whooshing noises. As she laughed in delight, spraying bits of chocolate and peanut over the armchair, Lottie looked on in disgust at the woman who was supposed to take care of her.

Sometimes Lottie felt more like a grown-up than her mum. Adults were, after all, supposed to look after children, but often Lottie was the one who dealt with the important things.

Mrs Parsons had never been what you

could call kind to Lottie. She tolerated her, but since Lottie's dad went to the shop last year for a bottle of milk and never returned, Mrs Parsons had grown more and more unkind towards her only daughter.

Lottie's mum had not been outside the house since Dad left, except to go to the garden to ask Sylvia next door to send her a new life on Liquorice Legend.

Since her mum's obsession with games began, their home had become very messy, and Lottie was finding that she had to prepare her own meals. It wouldn't be too bad, except that she didn't get to choose what she cooked.

Lottie's family didn't have as much money as the other children she went to school with. Instead of real food, Mrs Parsons liked to order lots of chocolate from FreshFoods online, which she would hide from everyone else. Her favourites were Creme Eggs and so around Easter time she became a little less unpleasant. But not much.

Lottie and her parents had moved in with her grandpa a couple of years ago. Things weren't too bad at first but, since Dad had left, it was becoming more difficult to cope. As well as her weekly school homework, Lottie had to make beds, cook meals, hoover, dust, wash up and do just about every other chore that you can think of that you *really* hate. As well as all her chores, Lottie had to take care of her grandpa, who had turned seventy-two a week ago. Looking after Gramps was the only thing that Lottie *didn't* hate about home, though.

Gramps didn't talk very often. He used to. In fact, Lottie had fond memories of when she was very young and would laugh with her grandparents until she cried. But, since Grandma died two years ago, his sadness at the loss of his wife had taken over him.

Put simply, he was now a very sad, lonely old man.

Lottie suspected that the medicine the doctors had given him for his weak arteries was really a fix for his broken heart. And she wanted to help mend it.

Every morning, she would get up early to make his breakfast. Every evening, she would bring his tablets with a glass of milk and sit with him while he ate the dinner that she had lovingly prepared for him. She went to bed late, woke up tired and most of the time arrived late to school. But she was determined that if she showed him enough care and attention, Gramps would return to his old self one day.

Lottie found the moments she spent with her grandfather were the most peaceful times in her day and gave her the chance to talk to someone about her problems at school, mainly involving Penelope. She told him about the times Penelope left her out of games on purpose, and the horrible nicknames she invented, like 'Lottie the Potty' or 'Grotty Lottie'. Occasionally he might respond with the odd word or two, but most of the time Lottie would find her grandpa staring into space. For some reason, however, Lottie always felt that he was listening.

As it turns out, she was right. Again. That's three times now, isn't it?

Gramps listened to everything.

'Vegetables,' Grandpa repeated as Lottie brought in his food and medicine that evening.

'No, Grandpa,' replied Lottie sadly. 'I'm sorry, not tonight. It's just the stew.'

He gulped down his tablets and placed the glass firmly on the table beside him. 'Big. Vegetables,' he repeated in a croaky voice.

'Gramps, I'm sorry. Mum didn't buy any this week, so . . .'

'No . . . big and small. Vegetables,' he tried again.

Lottie stood there, a look of bewilderment on her face.

'Your project! Big and Small?' he asked.

'Yes, Gramps . . . but you don't need to worry—' she tried to explain.

'Big! Vegetables!' he interrupted. 'You should grow an enormous vegetable for your project,' he went on, with a hint of excitement in his voice.

'Well . . .' Lottie began in surprise,

34

because these were the most words he had spoken in months!

'Yes, that's definitely what we'll do.' He continued to mutter to himself and then, looking Lottie in the eye, he whispered, 'That Penny wots-her-name won't win the prize this year. '

'Penelope?' Lottie questioned in disbelief, amazed that he really *had* been listening all this time.

'Yes. Her. The girl who's mean to you all the time. We'll teach her. You're going to win that project this year, my dear. You mark my words.'

Lottie tried to let him down gently. 'It's

a good idea, Gramps, if we had a whole school year,' she said quietly, 'but there are only thirty-four days left until the end of term and I doubt we can grow a vegetable big enough to compete with anything that Penelope's experts come up with.'

Grandpa's eyes glittered mischievously. 'Thirty-four days? That's plenty of time!' he exclaimed, and the largest smile Lottie had seen in two years spread across his face.

'But how . . .?' Lottie stared at him, confused.

'You leave that to me, my girl!'

36

And with that, Grandpa tapped his nose, got out of his special chair, walked to the back of the garden and disappeared into the shed.

FOUR

The shed was empty.

Lottie had raised her hopes. She had
allowed herself to get a teeny bit excited
that Grandpa might have a solution to her
project problem, and she half expected to
follow him into the shed to find a giant

vegetable already growing.

But she was wrong.

Well, you can't be right all the time, I suppose, otherwise you'd be a know-it-all and people don't like know-it-alls very much.

Anyway, the shed was empty. Apart from spiders. Lottie didn't like spiders very much. A few weeks ago, Penelope had managed to bribe a boy from Year Four to put a big spider in Lottie's lunch box. It frightened her so much that she fell backwards off her seat in the dinner hall and everyone had laughed at her. She still hadn't got over it.

Gramps was muttering something about a floorboard as he stamped his slippered feet along the floor, crouching low to the ground so that he looked like he was performing a street dance.

At first, she thought he was trying to kill the spiders, or perhaps he finally *had*

turned crazy! But as Lottie continued to watch him, it became clear that Grandpa was listening very carefully for something.

And then came the noise he had been waiting for.

A loud springing sound echoed around the walls of the shed, causing the spiders to scuttle to the corners. Grandpa stamped his foot again, harder this time, and there was the same noise.

Lottie watched in wonder as the seventy-two year-old man, who only yesterday had been confined to a chair, lowered himself to his knees and began to feel around the dirty floor with his hands. When his fingers reached the edge of the floorboard, he stopped suddenly and turned to Lottie. 'Stand back,' he said seriously.

Lottie did as she was told, took a stride backwards and positioned herself in the doorway of the stinky shed.

Grandpa pushed hard on the edge of the floorboard; the opposite side sprung up suddenly and hit a knot of wood on the roof before falling back to the floor. Then another strange noise – like a ping-pong ball bouncing back and forth – came from the ceiling, getting louder and louder until a wooden drawer popped out from the

43

wall like a cuckoo clock!

'It worked! I knew it would still be here!' Grandpa exclaimed as he walked quickly to the drawer to pull it out from the hole in the wall.

'This, my dearest,' he said, rubbing his hands together gleefully, 'is everything we are going to need to help us with your project!'

Lottie looked into the drawer as Gramps placed it carefully on the floor of the shed. By now, she had forgotten all about the spiders and sat down cross-legged to explore the contents of the mystery compartment.

44

Inside, Lottie could see a series of newspaper clippings and old Polaroid photographs. There was one of those things that doctors use to listen to your chest that Lottie couldn't quite remember the name of, and a little black book with pieces of paper stuffed inside. As Gramps rummaged further, he pulled out a harmonica, a small red tin and a strange contraption that Lottie didn't recognise.

'What's that?' Lottie asked, picking it up.

'That, my dear, is a Muzzlescrump!'

'A *what*?' Lottie said, trying to contain her laughter.

45

'A Muzzlescrump. That is what is going to help us make your vegetable enormous!' he said, picking up the thin silver device from the box. 'In fact, all of these things are going to help us. Now, have you decided what you'd like to grow yet?'

But Lottie wasn't listening any more. Instead, she was focused on the faces that were staring up at her from the photographs at the bottom of the drawer.

She reached inside to pull out the newspaper clippings that had turned yellow and brittle with age. LOCAL COUPLE WIN PRIZE FOR GIGANTIC

SWEDE! read one headline. **ONE GIANT LEEK FOR MANKIND!** said another. **UNBE-LEAF-ABLE! WORLD'S BIGGEST CABBAGE GROWN IN 22 DAYS!**

Each article had a picture of her grandparents in their younger years either standing next to, holding or sitting on top of enormous vegetables. There were photographs of massive cauliflowers and beetroots, and an image of Grandpa holding up a huge butternut squash. In one photograph, Gran was pictured trying to feed an abnormally large carrot to a giant rabbit!

Lottie glanced up to find her grandpa
staring at the pictures over her shoulder.
There was a mix of sadness and happiness
in his eyes.

'Those were the days,' he said softly.
'Your grandmother was the best vegetable

grower I have ever seen. She would have loved to have helped you with your project, Lottie.'

'But you're in these pictures too, Gramps,' she said, gazing back at him.

'Yes, we worked well as a team – but it was your gran that had the real talent. She had a way of understanding what the vegetables needed. She wrote it all down in here.' Gramps handed Lottie a black book that was stuffed with papers. Inside were pencil-written instructions for each type of vegetable: what it liked to eat, the kind of entertainment it required, the sort of environment it needed to thrive. There

49

were scribbled-out notes and diagrams, and little hints and tips added in different handwriting down the sides.

Lottie stared at her grandpa in disbelief; all this time he had kept his achievements hidden in a drawer in his stinky old shed.

'So what do all these things do then?' Lottie asked. 'And what do we do with a Muzzlescrump?'

Grandpa tapped his nose again. 'All in good time, little Lottie. First you need to decide what you would like to grow!'

'*LOTTIE!*' a voice boomed from the house through to the garden. 'Did you eat my last chocolate bar?'

'Better go, Gramps, or Mum will be on to us,' she said, skipping to the entrance of the shed.

FIVE

Lottie woke up the next morning to the smell of bacon cooking. She rubbed her eyes, pushed the thick brown curls from her face and dragged herself out of bed to find out where the smell was coming from.

As usual, she found her mum fast asleep on the settee, snoring loudly. A line of drool was dripping from the corner of her mouth on to the mobile phone that she still had clasped in her hand.

Lottie pushed open the door to the kitchen to discover her grandpa dancing around with frying pans. Two places were set at the table and Gramps was serving up a fried egg on to each plate. His face was bright red and the little bit of hair he had left was stuck to his head with sweat.

'Good morning, young lady. I thought *I* might cook the breakfast today,' he said cheerfully.

47

Lottie looked down at the plate of very crispy bacon, burnt toast and an egg that was dripping with oil.

'Gramps . . . this is . . . errr . . .?' Lottie struggled to find the words. She pinched herself to check whether this was all a dream. Almost overnight, Grandpa had returned to his old self!

'I know *you* normally make the breakfast,' he said, sitting down at the table and tucking a piece of paper towel over his bow tie and into the collar of his shirt, 'but I think it's about time that we started to share out the work in the Parsons household!'

He picked up his knife and fork and looked at Lottie, placing his hand on top of hers. 'You've looked after me for a long time, my dearest girl,' he said gently. 'Now it's time for us to look after each other.'

Lottie found that she was able to eat her breakfast, wash and dress with plenty of time to spare. She even found time to brush her hair properly!

When she arrived early at the school gates, Mrs Murray was standing on playground duty, warming her hands with a cup of coffee. She saw Lottie walking up the footpath towards her and almost dropped her mug! Checking her watch,

she looked again at
Lottie and her mouth
fell wide open like a
big fish. Lottie flashed
a cheeky grin at her
teacher as she strolled
into the playground,
only to walk straight
into Penelope and her
gaggle of admirers.

She put her head down and walked
past them quietly, trying not to draw
attention to herself, but Penelope's foot
flew out quickly, causing Lottie to trip and
fall awkwardly to the ground.

'Pay attention to where you are walking, Paaarsons!' Penelope screeched, her eyes narrowing so that she looked even meaner than usual. 'We were just discussing what we all plan to do for our school project. What's yours going to be, Grotty Lottie?'

Lottie tried desperately to keep it to herself but she wanted to see the look on Penelope's face when she realised she might actually have some competition for the prize this year. 'I'm going to grow a giant vegetable,' Lottie said proudly. 'My grandpa is going to help me. He thinks we might be able to break a record.'

'A giant vegetable!' Penelope snorted with laughter. 'Trust Lottie the Potty to come up with something so stupid. Don't you realise you're not going to have time? We've only got five weeks of term left, in case you hadn't noticed! It takes ages to grow vegetables.'

'What are you going to grow? A giant sprout, in time for Christmas!' squealed Ambrosia Anderson, Penelope's best friend, as the two of them faced each other, laughing and clapping their hands like excited sea lions.

Lottie felt a knot of anger in her stomach. There was no one she hated

more than Penelope. 'No, actually I'm going to grow . . .' Lottie racked her brains to think of vegetables, '. . . a parsnip,' she said finally.

'A paaarsnip?' Penelope sneered. 'That really is the silliest idea in the world. They don't even grow very big!'

'No, actually . . . it will be a pepper,'

Lottie corrected herself.

'A pepper or a paaarsnip – *whatever*! Neither one will grow big enough to win,' sneered Penelope, looking at her group of friends for moral support.

'Or, actually,' Lottie added, taking another stride backwards to avoid being so close to Penelope and her followers, 'a pumpkin might have potential.'

'A potential pumpkin?' Penelope spat. 'Well, make up your mind, Grotty! Is it a pumpkin, a pepper or a paaarsnip?' she screeched after Lottie, as Lottie walked away proudly.

Lottie strolled into her classroom, got

out her reading book and sat down at her
table next to William, who was reading a
magazine about dinosaurs.

'Hi, Lottie,' he said brightly, keeping
his eyes fixed on the magazine. 'I'm

researching facts for my project. Did you know that the smallest dinosaur egg that has ever been discovered is only three centimetres long?'

'Hmmm?' Lottie looked up from her reading book, her eyes focusing on last month's Hallowe'en display, which was littered with designs for pumpkin carvings.

A pumpkin seems like as good a vegetable as any, she thought to herself.

Penelope's teasing had only made her more determined to win the prize. If Grandpa really was as good at vegetable growing as he said, then this might be her chance to shine.

She couldn't wait to get home to tell Gramps.

Tomorrow was Saturday, which meant they had a whole weekend to make a start on Project Pumpkin.

Six

'The first thing we need is some hedgehog poo!' Grandpa announced as Lottie peered round the door of the shed the following morning.

She had returned home the previous afternoon excited to tell Gramps her decision about which vegetable to grow. Over dinner, they discussed the project in detail and made some important rules:

1) They would grow a large pumpkin.

2) They would hide it in the shed.

Yes, I know, there weren't many rules, but they were important all the same.

They agreed to prepare the soil the following day. Grandpa said that the preparation phase was a key part and couldn't be rushed. 'Fail to prepare and you prepare to fail,' he told Lottie. So they spent the rest of the evening drinking hot chocolate and chatting until very late.

Gramps described all the different
vegetables he had grown in different
places around the world: Aubergines

67

in Amsterdam, Cauliflowers in Cairo, Horseradishes in Helsinki, Broccoli in Bratislava and Onions in Oslo. He told Lottie all about how he and Gran had developed their secret formulas based on all of the different tips from the people they had met on their travels.

Lottie awoke late the next morning to find that Grandpa was already in the shed. He had removed several of the floorboards, had filled the hole with a deep layer of earth and was busy pinning up bits of paper to the back wall.

'I've been up all night, trying to find one . . .' Grandpa said as Lottie stepped carefully around the mound of soil.

'Trying to find what?' she said sleepily.

'A hedgehog!' he cried.

'What on earth for?' she asked in confusion.

'We need its poo!' shouted Grandpa. 'If we can't get enough poo for the soil then the pumpkin simply won't grow. And if we can't find a hedgehog, then we can't get the poo!'

Lottie looked around the garden at the piles of mess that next door's cat had left behind. There was certainly plenty of that.

'Couldn't we use a different animal?' Lottie asked. 'Like a cat? We've got mountains of cat poo.'

Grandpa ripped off a piece of paper from the wall and held it under Lottie's nose. On it were Grandma's neatly written Instructions for Growing the Perfect Pumpkin.

He pointed at the line that read:

Prepare the soil two days before planting the seed.

Planting material should be nine parts garden soil mixed evenly with one part hedgehog manure.

Lottie's heart sank. They needed at least three days to prepare the ground and plant the seed, which left less than thirty

70

days for the pumpkin to grow! If they couldn't get the right ingredients soon, then there would be no point in trying.

Hedgehogs were hard enough to spot at the best of times, so it was doubtful they would be able to just find one in the garden. Lottie remembered visiting an animal sanctuary once with her parents when she was very young. They had hedgehogs there, but that was miles away.

Lottie sighed heavily. It was game over. They had faced the first hurdle and couldn't get past it. She would have to find something else for her project instead.

Lottie looked at the pages that Gramps had ripped from the little black book. 'Never mind, Gramps,' she said, trying to sound cheerful. 'It was worth a go! Why don't we try growing something else instead?'

And then she noticed that Gran had written very faintly in pencil:

Hedgehog poo preferred, but the droppings of any spiky-haired creature will work.

Almost immediately, she had a solution to their problem.

'I think I know what to do, Gramps,' she declared. 'I'll be back in an hour.'

She grabbed her coat, slammed
the gate and ran all the way to William's
house.

SEVEN

'Has your dad
still got his baby
porcupine?' Lottie
said breathlessly as
William opened the
door.

'Errr, yes. He's cleaning out its enclosure as we speak,' William replied, surprised to see his schoolfriend on the doorstep.

'I need a poo,' Lottie continued, trying to get her breath.

'Oh, well, you'd better come in then,' said William. 'The toilet is up the stairs, second door on the—'

'No,' Lottie correctly him quickly. '*I* don't actually need to *do* a poo. I need a poo. From the porcupine. It's a long story.'

Lottie explained the plan to William. She told him about the things she and Gramps had found in the shed, about her grandpa's idea to beat Penelope by growing a massive pumpkin, and she showed him the piece of paper with her gran's carefully written notes.

William looked impressed. 'Wow, Lottie, if this works you might actually win. You might actually beat Penelope!'

The two friends loitered in the kitchen, waiting for William's dad to take his morning coffee break. William's father had forbidden his son from entering the porcupine enclosure, worried that he might get spiked. William also wasn't allowed to have friends over from school because Mr Winkleman was afraid that he might be reported for keeping exotic animals in his back garden.

If they wanted to get the poo, they would need to be very sneaky.

When the digital clock on the microwave flicked over to 11 a.m., William hid Lottie under a pile of clothes in the washing basket and grabbed one of his mum's plastic measuring jugs. Right on cue, Dad strolled in and switched the kettle on, whistling to himself as he trudged upstairs to the toilet. Lottie tried to keep as still as possible so as not to be discovered.

When Mr Winkleman was out of

earshot, William seized his chance. He ran swiftly into the garden and hurdled over the makeshift fence of the enclosure. The porcupine, not used to seeing a stranger in his home, stared

suspiciously. William maintained eye contact, just as he had seen his dad do, and slowly crept towards the poo pile. The porcupine watched, its nose twitching, as William scooped up a big mound of fresh poo into the jug.

Slowly, it began to assume its attack position, raising up its prickly bum in preparation to spike.

But William was too quick. He leapt over the fence and ran back into the kitchen and carefully placed the jug of poo on the table, just as his father strolled through the door.

'What's that, William?' asked Mr Winkleman as he spooned coffee and sugar into a mug and filled it with boiling water from the kettle.

William stared at the jug on the table, speechless for a moment. 'Er . . .' he stuttered, 'it's . . . er . . . it's chocolate brownie mix. I just thought I might have a go at baking something to take into school.'

'Ooooh, I love brownies!' declared William's dad excitedly, holding his finger out to dip it into the jug of poop.

'NO! DAD!' shouted William, surprising his father. 'I mean . . . It's just . . . your hands are probably dirty from the porcupine cleaning and I . . . er . . . don't want you to try the brownies until they're finished. If you don't mind.'

'Suit yourself.' Disappointed, Mr Winkleman shrugged and walked back to the garden.

Lottie could barely contain her laughter as William flung off the clothes to free her from the dirty washing.

He handed her the measuring jug and Lottie threw her arms around him, almost smothering him with her mane of curls.

'Thank you so much,' she whispered. William looked a little embarrassed but an uneven smile crossed his lips. 'It's OK, Lottie, don't mention it. But you'd better go quickly, before he comes back and wants to taste it again!'

As she walked home, carrying a big jug of steaming poo, Lottie began to imagine the look on Penelope's face when she found out that she hadn't won the school project this year.

She was daring to hope that her imagination might become reality.

The porcupine poo worked like a dream.

'Such a clever girl,' Gramps had said to Lottie as they added the poo to the soil and picked out the oval-shaped pumpkin pip from Grandpa's special red tin of seeds.

They soaked it in orange juice for two days while waiting for the poo to mix with the soil. Gramps allowed Lottie to do the planting. The seed had to go exactly fifteen centimetres into the ground (Lottie used her school ruler to measure this) and it needed to be watered with four two-litre bottles of Irn-Bru which Grandpa had bought in advance.

Once planted, Grandma's instructions demanded that they leave the seed in complete darkness for a whole day.

While they waited to find out whether it took root, Lottie and Gramps spent the evening preparing the next stage of the plan, which they codenamed Operation Enormous.

They consulted the pumpkin-growing guidelines. Which you can see below:

Instructions for Growing the Perfect Pumpkin

Pumpkins should be planted at the beginning of spring and harvested during the months of autumn. If choosing to grow outside pumpkin season, vegetables should be kept undercover at all times to avoid frostbite.

Soil preperation

- Prepare the soil two days before planting the seed
- Planting material should be <u>nine</u> parts garden soil mixed evenly with <u>one</u> part hedgehog manure

Hedgehog poo preferred but the droppings of any spiky-haired creature will work

Best shape

Seed preperation and planting

- Choose biggest seed available → *Look for pale colour*
- Soak seed in fresh orange juice for two days before planting.
- Plant seed exactly 15cm into soil.
- Water immediately with orange-coloured fizzy drink *(Approx 8 litres or 14 pints)*
- Leave seed in complete darkness for one day

The one with bits left in

Irn-Bru best but orangeade suitable

Ingredients

4 parts baked beans
2 parts sprouts ← *Frozen or fresh*
2 parts chewing gum
2 parts Marmite
1 part sugar-free mints ◯ *(Not too strong)*

Must be chewed in advance

Water regularly with chosen <u>fizzy drink</u> – can be watered down if necessary

Entertainment

Individual pumpkins will require variations of the following:

Harmonica songs *Rock songs preferred*

Poetry

Due to trouble sleeping, pumpkin may need comforting in early evening/night with lullabies, warm drinks, cuddles.

Hot choc
Milk with honey

You will notice from these guidelines that pumpkins, like all vegetables, require a very special diet. You will also know – if you've been lucky enough to be allowed to carve one for Hallowe'en – that pumpkins are almost completely hollow inside.

During a trip to Panama in 1983, Grandma had discovered from a local farmer that the key to getting a pumpkin to achieve its maximum growth was making sure that it had enough air.

By air, I mean *gas*.

By gas, I mean *flatulence*.

Flatulence is a word people sometimes use for when they've got lots of trumps. Otherwise known as toots, bottom burps, parps, blow-offs, farts. So basically, Grandpa and Lottie needed to make sure that the pumpkin was brewing enough farts to make its insides expand.

Haven't you ever wondered why it smells so bad when you cut open a pumpkin?

Well, now you know.

From this discovery, Lottie's grandparents had developed a set of ingredients that would help the pumpkin expand rapidly.

Grandpa and Lottie made a special trip to FreshFoods, using Gramps's pension money to get the food the pumpkin

required. They put
ninety-six tins of baked
beans, thirty bags
of frozen sprouts,
eighteen packets
of apple-flavoured
chewing gum, a
hundred bottles of Irn-Bru, twelve jars

of Marmite and two tubes of
sugar-free mints through
the self-service checkout.
Grandpa had a little
trouble with the
technology and
said some rather

rude words
when the
robot lady's
voice kept
telling
him to
'Please place
the items

in the bagging area', but they got there
eventually. They even bought Mum a pack
of Screme Eggs – they're special Creme
Eggs they make for Hallowe'en, with
green icing inside.

Everything was in place. They just
had to wait patiently to see if the poo had

worked its magic. But as you will already know, it worked like a dream.

When they opened the door of the shed the next day, the pumpkin had not only taken root, it had grown to thirty centimetres and had tendrils over a metre long.

'It's working,' Lottie squealed in delight.

'What on earth did you expect?' said Gramps, putting an arm around his granddaughter.

They both stopped briefly and stared at their creation, savouring the moment together.

'What's that noise?' said Lottie, breaking the silence.

They stepped closer towards the pumpkin, which seemed to be emitting a low whistling sound, like an old-fashioned kettle that was just starting to boil.

'Why is it making that sound?' she questioned.

Grandpa grabbed the stethoscope from the box, put the eartips into his ears and held up the circular part to the pumpkin's skin, listening carefully to the noise.

'It's hungry,' said Gramps finally. 'It needs a good feeding.'

He turned to Lottie. 'Get the
ingredients, my girl. It's time to prepare
the Muzzlescrump.'

NINE

Grandpa pulled the stethoscope from his ears and retrieved the Muzzlescrump from the secret drawer while Lottie unwrapped the chewing gum and started chewing.

The Muzzlescrump consisted of a

short metal pipe with a round dial fixed to the top which had lots of complicated numbers. Gramps pushed a green button on the side and a large spike extended from the bottom of the pipe, which he used to secure it to the top of the pumpkin. When he pressed the button again, a further seven prongs appeared from the top of the dial, each one with a tiny metal cup. They curved upwards so that it looked like the frame of an umbrella when it gets turned inside out on a very windy day.

'This is where we put the food, Lottie,' he said as he filled up one of the cups

with Marmite. 'Vegetables either love or hate Marmite. If they love it then it does wonders for their growth. But if they hate it, it can kill them off quickly. Luckily, pumpkins fall into the first category.'

Lottie watched in fascination as her grandpa filled the cups with the required ingredients. He poured baked beans in one compartment, filled another with the defrosted sprouts, and a fourth was packed with the chewing gum that was now making Lottie's jaw ache.

This would give the pumpkin enough food for three days, and then it would require a refill.

'Why can't we just pour all the ingredients on to the soil?' asked Lottie, as Grandpa filled the last compartment with a couple of sugar-free mints. 'Why do we have to put it in the muzzulthingiemajig?'

'The Muzzlescrump, Lottie. Please say it properly. This device is what your gran and I used to help us win countless competitions,' said Grandpa. 'Firstly, it stops your ingredients going nombulant – that's a term us growers use for vegetable food that has gone rotten – but secondly, it makes sure you get the mixture absolutely perfect for the specific vegetable's needs.'

He guided Lottie towards the

pumpkin. 'Look at this.' He pointed
at the complicated dial on top of the
Muzzlescrump. 'These numbers are
used to set the quantities needed of each
ingredient to make the perfect mix.'

He consulted Grandma's notes and
twisted the dial five times back and forth
like a lock on a safe.

'Watch,' he said, pressing the green
button for a third time and stepping back.

The machine jerked unsteadily as
the prongs holding the metal cups were
sucked back inside the middle tube. Then
came a clicking noise followed by a quiet
buzzing and a wild spinning motion, as

the Muzzlescrump whirred into action, turning faster and faster for about thirty seconds, until it jolted to a halt.

The metal prongs slowly reappeared, this time downturned towards the soil, and a gloopy mixture seeped from them into the earth around the pumpkin. The Muzzlescrump rotated very slightly, the prongs moving in a crisscross motion, to ensure even coverage of the soil.

They watched as the tendrils of the pumpkin began to move on their own, lapping up the mixture.

Grandpa made a watering device from an old sprinkler system and attached it to a large bucket of Irn-Bru so that they could be sure the vegetable was getting everything it needed.

'So what do we do now?' Lottie said, brushing off the soil from her hands.

'Nothing,' replied Gramps. 'We wait.'

TEN

After thirteen days of growing, the pumpkin was already over a metre wide.

Due to its ever-increasing size, it required more attention every day and Gramps and Lottie soon worked out that certain noises meant that it needed something.

As the days passed, Grandpa listened carefully to the pumpkin with the stethoscope and spotted a pattern to its habits and behaviour. Every four hours it would start to make some kind of strange noise to indicate what it wanted.

In order to achieve maximum growth in a short time, Gramps created a rota system where he and Lottie would take turns to fulfil the pumpkin's needs. The rota was as follows:

103

8am	Low rumble	An up-tempo wake-up song played on the harmonica. It particularly likes the joys of Queen, especially 'Bohemian Rhapsody', which as Gramps has worked out, is rather difficult to play on the harmonica.
12noon	Irregular belching sounds	Poetry and news stories. The pumpkin is a fan of Wordsworth and likes broadsheets, not tabloids, which they discovered when they read the Sun out loud and it nearly exploded.
4pm	A high-pitched squeak	Massage and skin polishing.
8pm	Whistling	A selection of lullabies played on the harmonica. Warm milk and honey.
12midnight	Soft purring	Gentle stroking/cuddling.

They hadn't figured out what to do at 4 a.m., since neither Grandpa nor Lottie could be bothered to get out of bed.

Three weeks into Operation Enormous, the pumpkin was expanding *so* rapidly it was almost as big as the inside of the shed and was beginning to give off a foul odour.

On Day Twenty-five, Lottie was held up at school and was late for the 4 p.m. shift. She ran into the garden at 4.45 p.m. to find her mother finishing a conversation with Sylvia through the hole in the fence. The pumpkin was obviously in need of attention as the squeaking noise had reached a point where it could be heard outside the shed.

Lottie tried to tiptoe past her mum without her noticing.

'What are you sneaking around for?' said Mrs Parsons, squinting at her daughter suspiciously. 'Don't think I haven't noticed you and the old fogey

messing around in the garden. You're up
to something. I know it.'

'No, Mum,' said
Lottie innocently,
trying to hide the
massage oil behind
her back. 'I was just

looking for my skipping rope.'

'Well, do something useful,' barked Mum, walking back towards the house. 'There's a horrible smell coming from somewhere, and a funny noise out here. I think it must be the drains. Go and see if they're blocked and if they are, then sort them out.'

'We'll have to move it tonight,' agreed Grandpa when Lottie recounted the conversation with her mum later that evening. 'The smell is only going to get worse. The pumpkin's nearly the size of the shed anyway. I don't think anyone is going to beat that, Lottie.'

She smiled to herself. Even if she was a couple of days early delivering the finished product, she knew her teachers would be gobsmacked.

After dinner, when they were sure Mum was engrossed by her mobile phone games, Gramps and Lottie went out to the garden with a huge knife to cut the roots. Grandpa suggested that they should carve out a scary face on the front of the pumpkin, which Lottie thought was an excellent idea.

The pumpkin had surprisingly thin skin but it was so big that Lottie had to climb up on to Grandpa's shoulders to cut out the face.

They decided to model the features on Penelope by carving two little eyes, a thin smile and a rather large triangular nose. As Lottie plunged the knife in some of the gas inside escaped, so that it made a snorting sound, just like Penelope's laugh.

She won't be laughing tomorrow, thought Lottie.

As a finishing touch, Grandpa painted a sign on a large piece of wood that said:

From SMALL things,
BIG things grow
Project by Lottie Parsons — Class 3M

They would move it tonight under the cover of darkness and leave it outside the school gates for all to see in the morning.

ELEVEN

What happened next was a bit of a blur for Lottie because, if she was being very truthful, she found it all a little bit scary.

But I can assure you that she was a very brave girl indeed.

You see, what Lottie didn't know when

they began to transport the pumpkin that night, was that Grandpa had forgotten to take his medicine.

They had been so excited about everything that both of them failed to notice that the glass of milk and tablets that Lottie brought in for him every night still sat, untouched, on the little table next to Gramps's special chair.

They should've been in his tummy.

At around midnight, when Lottie and Grandpa were rolling a two-metre pumpkin up the hill towards school, Grandpa felt a strain in his left arm and an intense pain in the middle of his chest. They rested the pumpkin down for a moment so that Gramps could sit for a while to get his breath. The school gates were at the top of the hill. They were almost there and Lottie reckoned she was strong enough to do the last few metres alone. She turned to Gramps to tell him so.

But he had collapsed.

Lottie suddenly found herself alone, in the middle of the night, with no one to help her. Everything seemed to be happening in slow motion and she wasn't sure what to do . . .

Fortunately for Grandpa, Lottie came to her senses.

She dropped to her knees and placed her cheek above Grandpa's nose and lips, the way the St John Ambulance woman had taught her during Summer School. Then she rested her palm on Grandpa's tummy. She concentrated, but she couldn't feel any breath on her cheek, or any movement from his tummy. So she clasped her hands together and pressed as hard as she could . . .

The vibrations of this action, combined with a slight breeze that evening, caused the pumpkin to tilt slightly.

A slight tilt turned into a small topple.

A small topple turned into a big tumble.

The pumpkin began to roll.

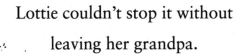

Lottie couldn't stop it without leaving her grandpa. It was him or the pumpkin.

I'm sure you have got to know Lottie well enough by now to know what she chose.

She continued to keep her grandpa's heart beating while she waited for someone, anyone, to help. But it was too late for the pumpkin; the humungous vegetable tumbled down the hill, slowly at first and then faster, gathering more and more speed. The shiny orange skin that she had lovingly polished every day began to flake off on the tarmac. Faster and faster it rolled, spinning awkwardly down the road, until it was stopped in its tracks by a police car at the bottom of the hill.

The pumpkin smashed into a thousand pieces against the police car, sending its stringy insides flying everywhere.

The remains lay scattered across the street like a pool of giant's sick and a strong smell of digested sprout wafted through the air.

A policeman, who very luckily wasn't in his car at the time, had to rub his eyes to check whether he was dreaming. Had a giant pumpkin just squashed his patrol car? He looked up in the direction of where it had appeared and noticed the figure of a little girl, desperately doing everything to keep her favourite person alive.

Running towards her, the policeman quickly understood the situation. He took over, requesting an ambulance on his radio receiver.

As the paramedics arrived, the policeman turned his attention to Lottie.

'What's your name, little girl?' he asked quietly.

'Lottie Parsons. I live at number twenty-six, Eastern Avenue,' she answered, as tears began to form in her eyes. 'Is my grandpa going to be OK?'

'I'm not sure,' he said sadly, 'but he was lucky that you were here.'

Then he cleared his throat. 'Is it my imagination or did I just see a giant pumpkin roll down the hill and smash into my car?' he asked Lottie.

'Yes,' she said, as a trickle ran down her cheek. 'It was my school project.'

Lottie didn't go to school the next day. She followed the ambulance to the hospital with the policeman, and the nurses let her sleep next to Gramps's bed because she didn't want him to be alone.

When the doctors arrived at 9 o'clock

the next morning, they explained to Lottie that Gramps was going to be OK. He would have to stay in hospital for a little while but would soon be back to his old self.

Lottie hung her head in shame. 'It's my fault,' she said, bursting into tears. 'If he hadn't been helping me with my stupid project then none of this would have happened!'

'Actually,' the doctor knelt down, 'it was probably your actions that saved your grandfather's life.' He handed Lottie a tissue. 'You've been a very brave girl and you should be extremely proud of yourself.'

When Grandpa finally stirred from his

long sleep a few hours later, Lottie listened as the nurses explained where he was.

'Yes, but what happened to the pumpkin?' She heard his muffled voice and peered round the curtain to see him.

'Lottie!' He held his arms open wide and they hugged so tightly that the nurse had to tell them to stop as it was causing the machines attached to Grandpa to bleep violently.

'I'm not going to school tomorrow, Gramps. I can't face Penelope winning the project again and I don't have anything to present,' Lottie said when she'd explained what had happened.

'You *will* go, my girl! You'll go and tell the teachers what happened. We haven't done all that work for nothing!'

'Yeah – I'll tell them everything, Grandpa, and they'll definitely believe me,' she said sarcastically.

'Just tell them the truth,' he said seriously. 'I'm not taking no for an answer.'

And so Lottie did what her grandpa

124

insisted she do. She strolled into school late the next morning, to find that all of the students and parents were already gathered in the hall. Nell Bear, the smallest girl in Year Three, was in the middle of explaining how she had constructed a giant matchstick model of the *Titanic* when Lottie slipped in through the back doors and found her place.

The next presentation, by Owen Tams, was about the Vatican City, the smallest country in the world; then came William's fact file about dinosaurs, which was actually quite interesting. Ambrosia Anderson had made a seven-tiered cake, which Mrs Murray was taking sneaky bites of, followed by Faith Sevier, who had grown a miniature garden in a shoe box, and Finlay Church, who showed off his prized collection of enormous teddy bears.

Lottie sat through presentation after presentation, knowing that her pumpkin would have beaten them all.

To add insult to injury, Penelope had stolen Lottie's idea and exhibited three oversized vegetables: a pepper, a parsnip and, you guessed it, a pumpkin. She had dressed herself in a farmer's outfit and read out a poem about her growing methods.

It was all lies. Her parents had obviously paid someone to do all the work.

Each of Penelope's vegetables measured just under a metre long and were tiny compared to what Lottie and Gramps had grown.

Lottie was so angry and upset she could barely get out the words when it was her turn to speak.

She stood up at the front of the assembly hall, her voice like a mouse's squeak.

'I'm afraid my project went horribly wrong this year,' she began, nervously. 'I had something really good but it didn't work out in the end.'

She heard the distinctive snort from Penelope and a few other giggles from the audience. She wanted the ground to swallow her up but she would settle for just being allowed to go back to her seat.

She looked pleadingly towards her teacher. 'May I sit down, Mrs Murray?'

'Not just yet, Lottie. I'd like to know a little more about what you were going to do, please,' she said through a mouthful of cake.

Lottie took a deep breath, her grandpa's words echoing in her ears:

Just tell the truth.

'Well,' she hesitated, 'I grew a giant pumpkin with my grandpa. We grew it with baked beans and sprouts and Irn-Bru. It was bigger than Penelope's, much bigger, but when we were bringing it to school, my grandpa had an accident and, well . . .'

'LIAR!' shouted a voice from the crowd. Penelope had stood up and was pointing at Lottie. 'She's a copycat! She stole my idea!'

The crowd of students gasped and the hall was suddenly silent.

And then Ambrosia Anderson stood up carefully from her seat.

'Well, you told me you were going to make a giant cake.' She scowled at Penelope. 'That's why I made one too. I thought mine would be bigger than yours. I didn't want you to win again this year!'

'Sit down, please, Ambrosia. You too, Penelope,' said Mr Dulland, the headteacher. 'Lottie, this seems a little too much of a coincidence. Have you got any evidence? A photo, perhaps? Of your giant pumpkin?'

Mr Dulland had the kind of look on his face that suggested he didn't believe Lottie but had to investigate the facts all the same.

'No, sir. I don't have a mobile phone to take any pictures and we kept it a secret in the shed. Even my mum doesn't know about it. We wanted it to be a surprise.'

'This is preposterous!' Mrs Pembleton-Puce exclaimed. 'That girl has clearly pinched my Penelope's idea! She is quite obviously a little copycat!'

'No, she didn't!' shouted Ambrosia. 'Lottie told Penelope what she was going to do weeks ago! Honest, Mr Dulland! If anyone's a copycat, it's Penelope.'

'It's true!' Now William was standing up too. 'Lottie came to my house for the porcupine poo to help her pumpkin grow!

My dad has one in his back garden!'

Mr Winkleman's face flushed as he tried to make his son sit down.

'I saw Lottie and her grandfather buying the ingredients!' said a mum in a FreshFoods uniform. 'I thought it was a bit weird why anyone would want that many baked beans!'

Slowly, the whispers in the assembly hall began to rise to shouts. Lottie could hear the word 'copycat' being passed around from student to student.

Soon a full-on chorus had broken out in the hall:

'Copycat!'

133

'Copycat!'

'Copycat!'

Lottie closed her eyes in dismay, knowing this was going to end badly.

But when she opened them again, she realised that everyone was pointing at Penelope, and not at her.

She had told the truth and people had believed her.

'Copycat!'

'Copycat!'

They continued to chant, getting louder and louder.

Penelope ran towards the front of the hall, where her mother was shouting

and making angry gestures towards Mr
Dulland.

'I'm not a copycat! I AM NOT!' she
screeched, stomping furiously towards
Ambrosia's cake. Carefully she picked up
the top tier, which was covered in a thick
layer of creamy icing.

A few at a time, the voices dwindled
and the hall fell silent again.

'SAY IT AGAIN! I DARE YOU!' she
screamed in anger, holding the top layer
of cake above her head, ready to launch
it at the first person who had the nerve to
challenge her.

Lottie tried to put herself in Penelope's

shoes and imagined how she might feel if she were in her situation. She stepped forward, away from the crowd of teasing students.

'It's OK, Penelope,' she said gently. 'If you say you didn't copy, then we believe you.' She smiled, holding out her hand in a gesture of friendship and forgiveness.

But Penelope was a very silly girl indeed.

'Oh shut up, Grotty Lottie!' she replied viciously. 'Nobody cares what you think anyway!' Taking aim, she raised the cake higher above her head in preparation to throw it at her target.

But the
cake was
too heavy
to hold.
Penelope
lost her
balance,
tripped
on a loose
straw from
her farmer's
costume and
toppled backwards into the remains of
Ambrosia's iced creation.

'She's in the cake!' shouted William,

running to Lottie's side as they watched
her struggle to free herself from the sticky
jam and sponge mix.

The whole school exploded into fits
of laughter as Mrs Pembleton-Puce, in an

attempt to help her daughter, slipped on some stray icing and toppled into the cake herself!

Mr Dulland tried to regain control but it was no use. The whole school hall descended into chaos.

It was probably the best day at school that Lottie had ever had.

THIRTEEN

Just so you know, Lottie won the school project. It wasn't a big prize, just a nice box of fancy chocs (which Lottie gave to her Mum). The real reward, however, was the sense of pride and achievement that Lottie felt inside, and the wonderful relationship she now had with her grandpa. Even Mum was proud. And *very* pleased with the chocolates.

It turns out that the policeman who had witnessed the giant pumpkin went into school the following day to tell Mr Dulland everything that had happened, even showing him the big dent in his police car. They couldn't prove the pumpkin existed, but Lottie won nevertheless. The teachers said her enormous act of bravery was enough to justify giving her the prize.

Penelope's parents removed their daughter from Maplebrook Primary and are currently trying to claim compensation for the emotional effects that the cake incident has had on their daughter. Lottie enjoys school a little more now.

Grandpa also made a full recovery and together they are helping Mum to get out more.

They all look after each other a little better these days. Lottie reminds Grandpa to take his medicine every night, and Grandpa makes sure Lottie gets to school on time every morning and helps her with her homework. Mum has limited the time she spends on Liquorice Legend to two hours a day and has even started to share her secret stash of chocolate! If she's having a good day, she hoovers too.

Lottie and Gramps have kept up the growing and are currently trying to break the record for the world's largest avocado, which Gramps has never grown before. He thinks Lottie has got Grandma's special talent for vegetable growing.

As for Lottie, well, she's a lot happier too. In fact, you might say that her confidence has blossomed.

Just like the pumpkin.

Just like Grandpa.

But I guess that's what happens when you give things a little bit of care and attention.

Lottie was right.

There she goes again – little know-it-all!

THE END

ACKNOWLEDGEMENTS

In many ways, writing and publishing a book is a lot like growing an enormous pumpkin – it has its own very special recipe. In the case of this book, the following people were vital to my recipe and deserve a big thank you.

A solid foundation soil: Mum, who passed on to me a very small fraction of her creativity; Dad, who read to me every night and made up fantastic stories on demand; and my fantastic English teacher, who told me my writing was good.

The right environment: A household full of love, craziness and encouragement should suffice. A big sister and brother to take care of you and give you confidence also helps, as well as the support of a remarkable husband. The best ones are called Luke; they make you laugh lots and keep you in the right frame of mind for writing children's books.

The perfect seed: Hachette and ITV's *Lorraine* for providing such a fantastic opportunity.

Polishing and preparation: I'd highly recommend the experts at Hodder Children's Books who are very skilled in this area, especially: Anne McNeil, Polly Lyall Grant, Katie Price and Alison Padley. Your advice and guidance have been absolutely essential both for the growth of this book and the growth of me as a writer.

Beautification and presentation: Sarah Jennings, who has made my characters come to life with her superb illustrations.

Getting my story published means more to me than anyone will ever understand and so to anyone who has contributed to that process in any way, I thank you from the bottom of my heart.

Sarah Jennings is a freelance illustrator currently living in the Midlands. At a very young age she discovered a love of drawing and has been scribbling and sketching ever since. Since studying illustration and graduating in 2013, she has worked on a variety of children's books. Sarah works from her home studio in the company of Pea, her very old but very naughty cat. You can see more of her work at sarahjenningsillustration.com

By the real Lottie Parsons,
the inspiration for this story